PEACOCK PUNKS

Dale Lazarov, Mauro Mariotti & Janos Janecki

PEACOCK PUNKS

Script and art direction by Dale Lazarov
Line art by Mauro Mariotti
Color art by Janos Janecki
©2015 Dale Lazarov & Mauro Mariotti // All rights reserved.

StickyGraphicNovels.com

Printed and distributed by
ComicMix, LLC.,
71 Hauxhurst Ave. Suite B
Weehawken, NJ 07086
http://www.comicmix.com

Hardcover ISBN: 9781939888587

BUS
1 7 51 60

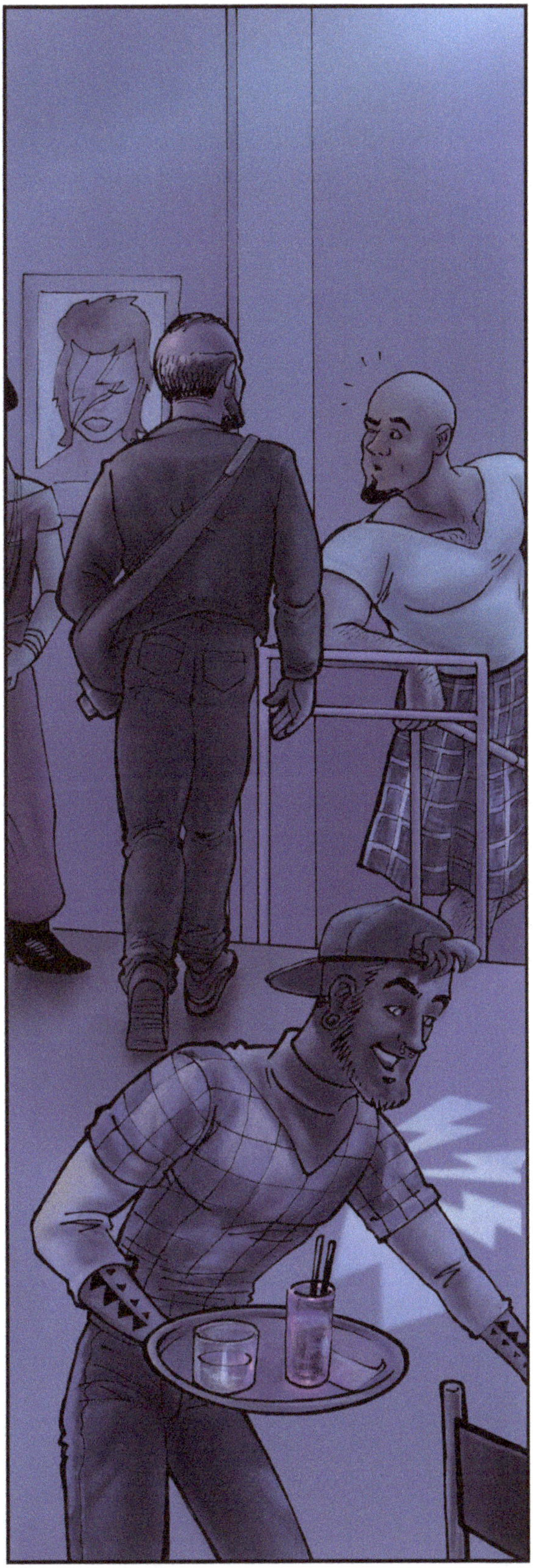

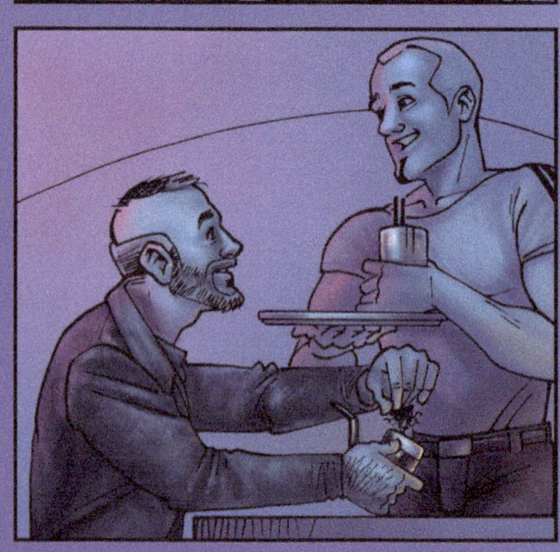

OGILVY ON ADVERTISING

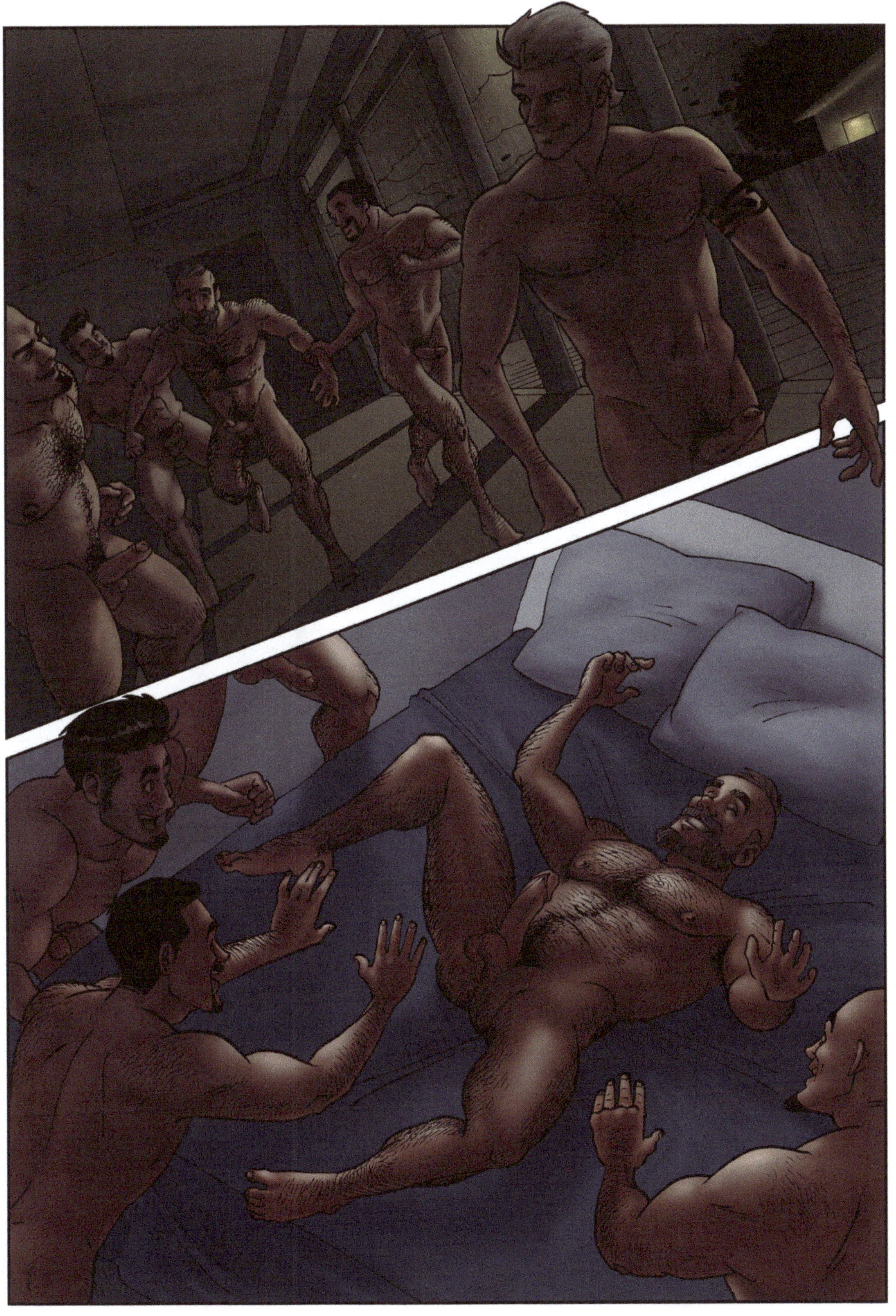

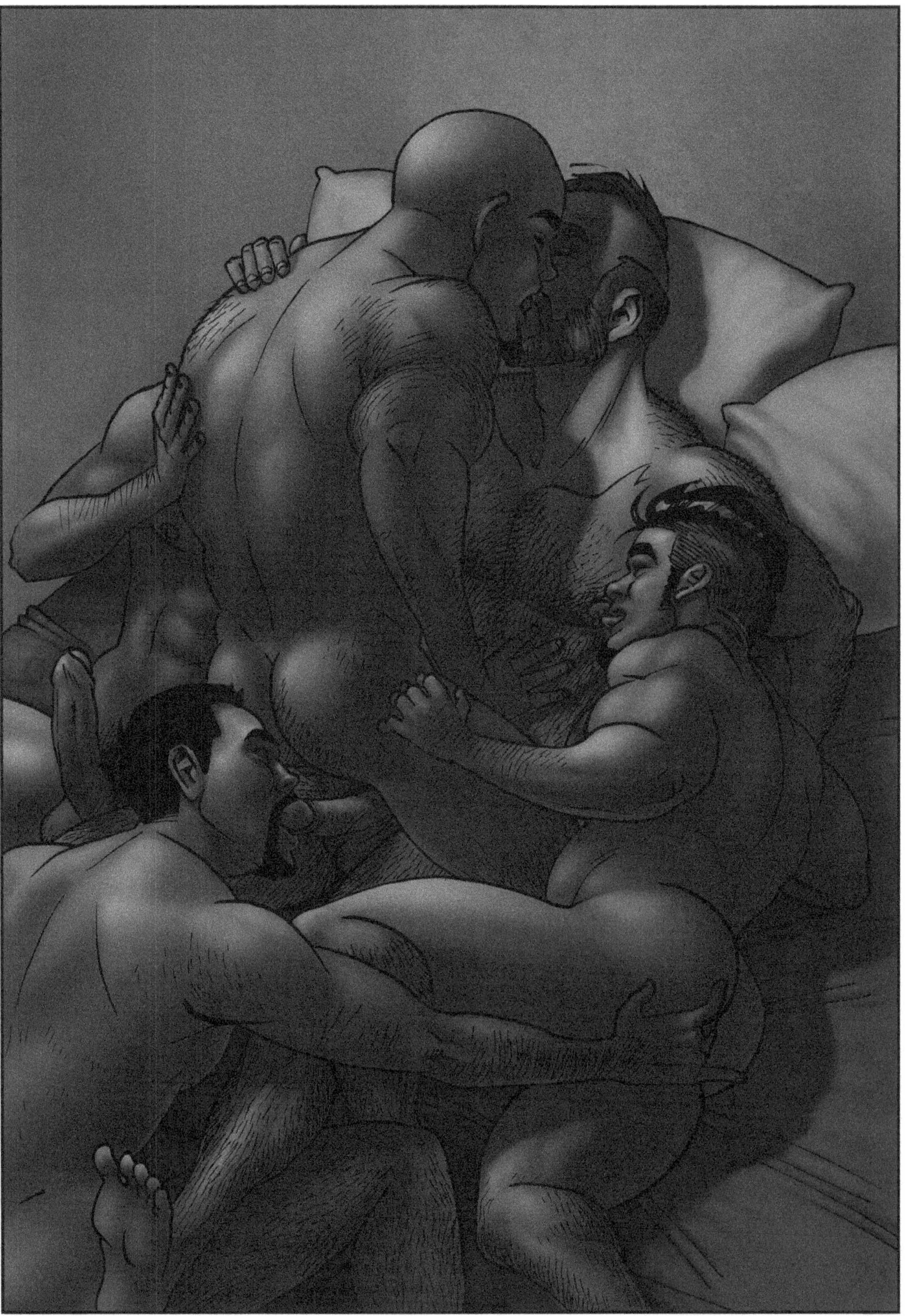

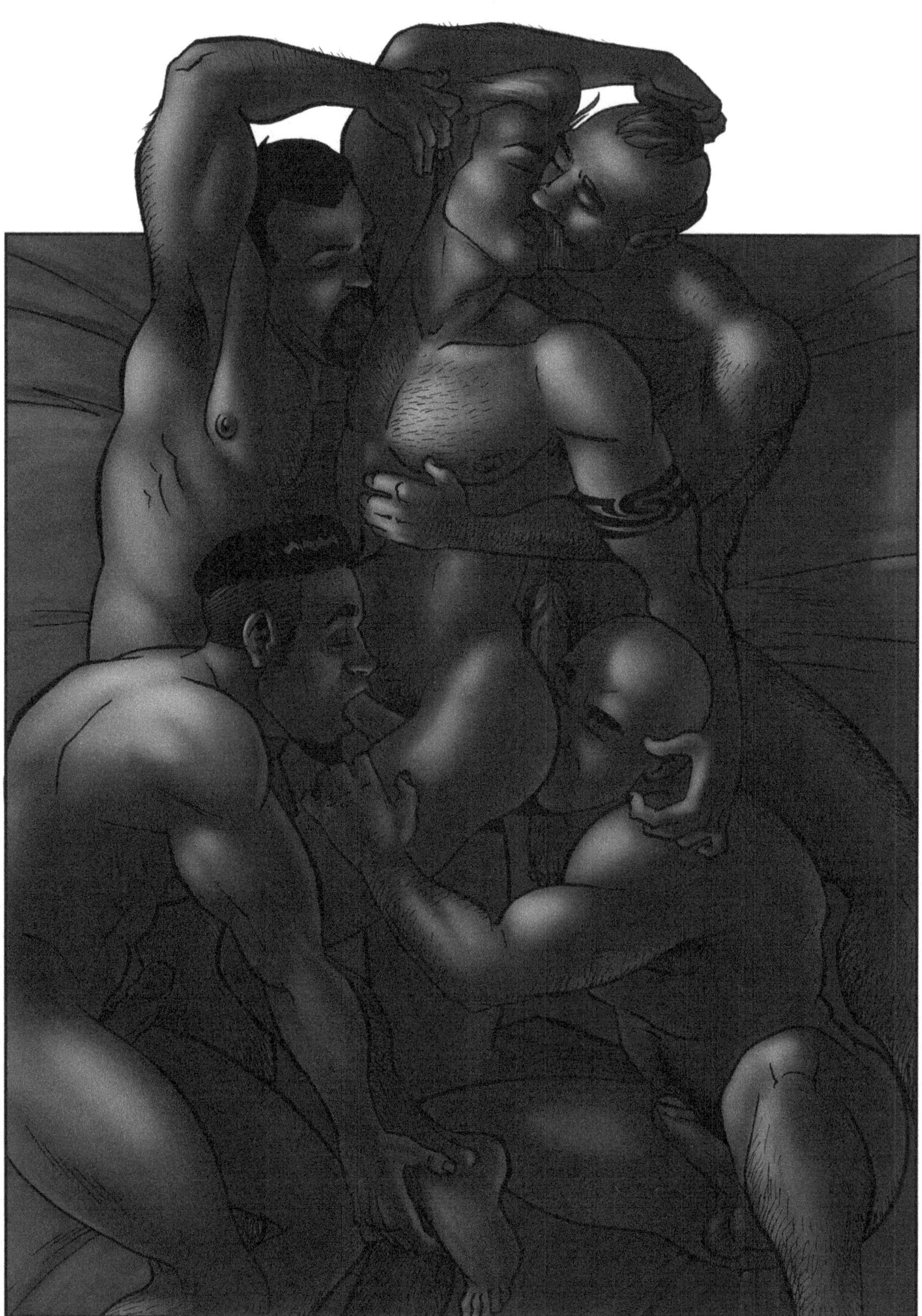

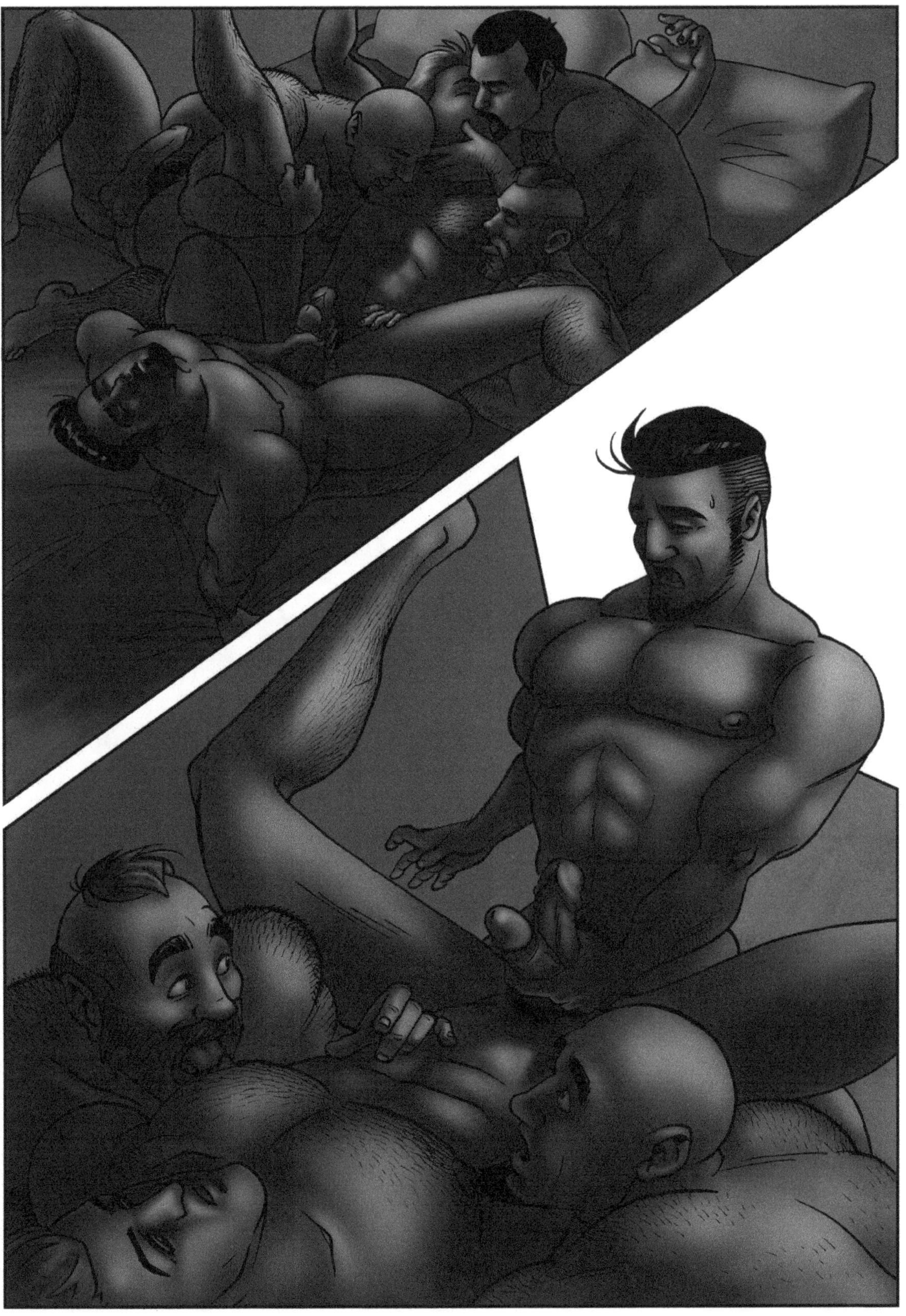

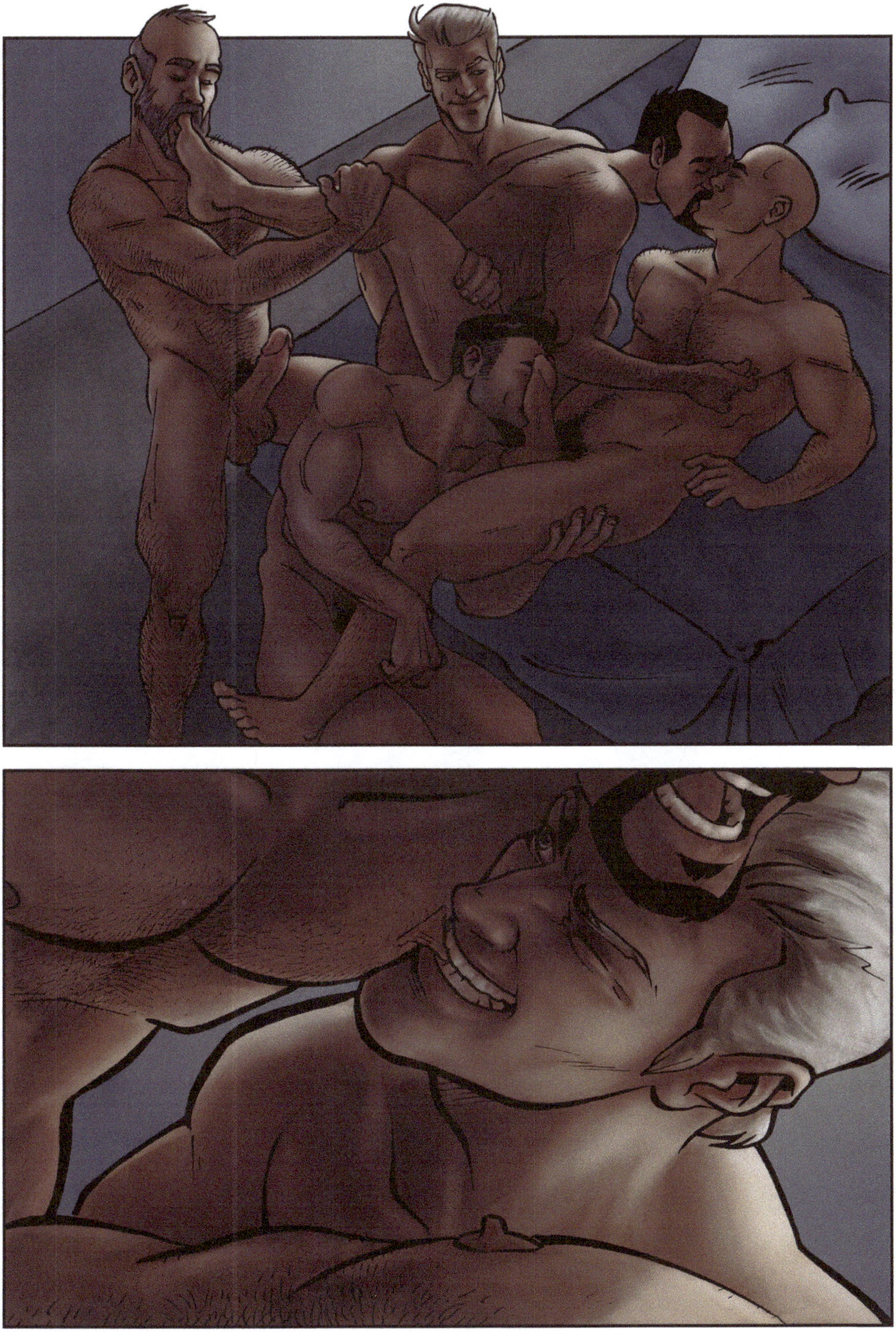

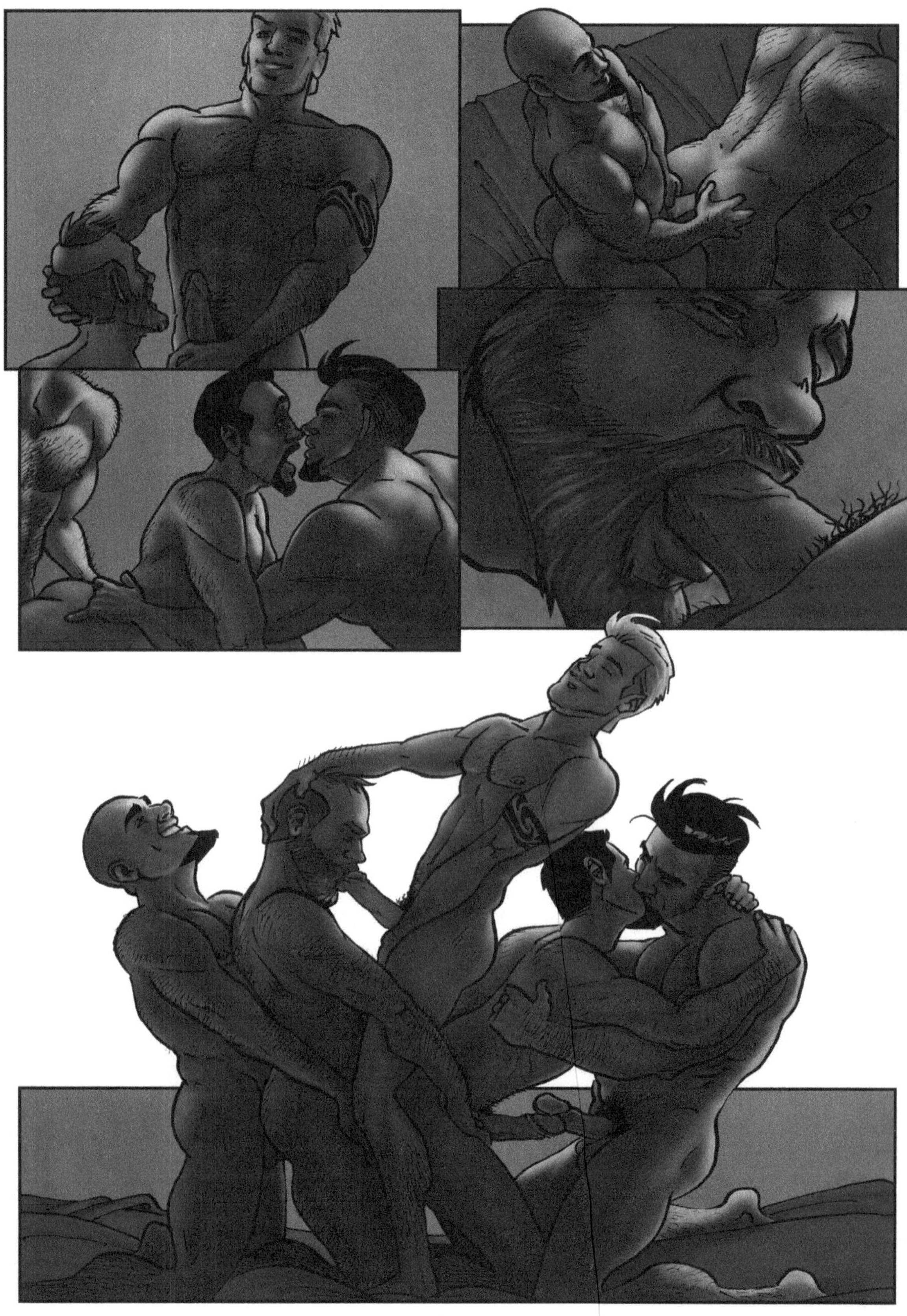

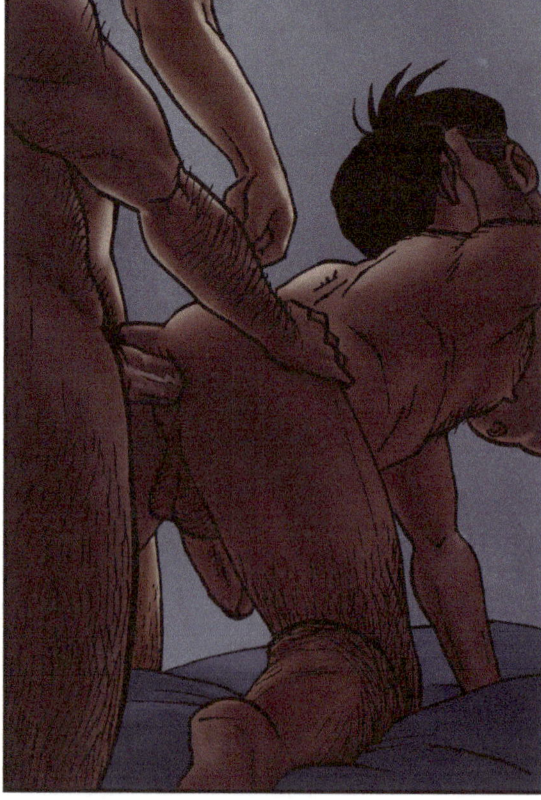

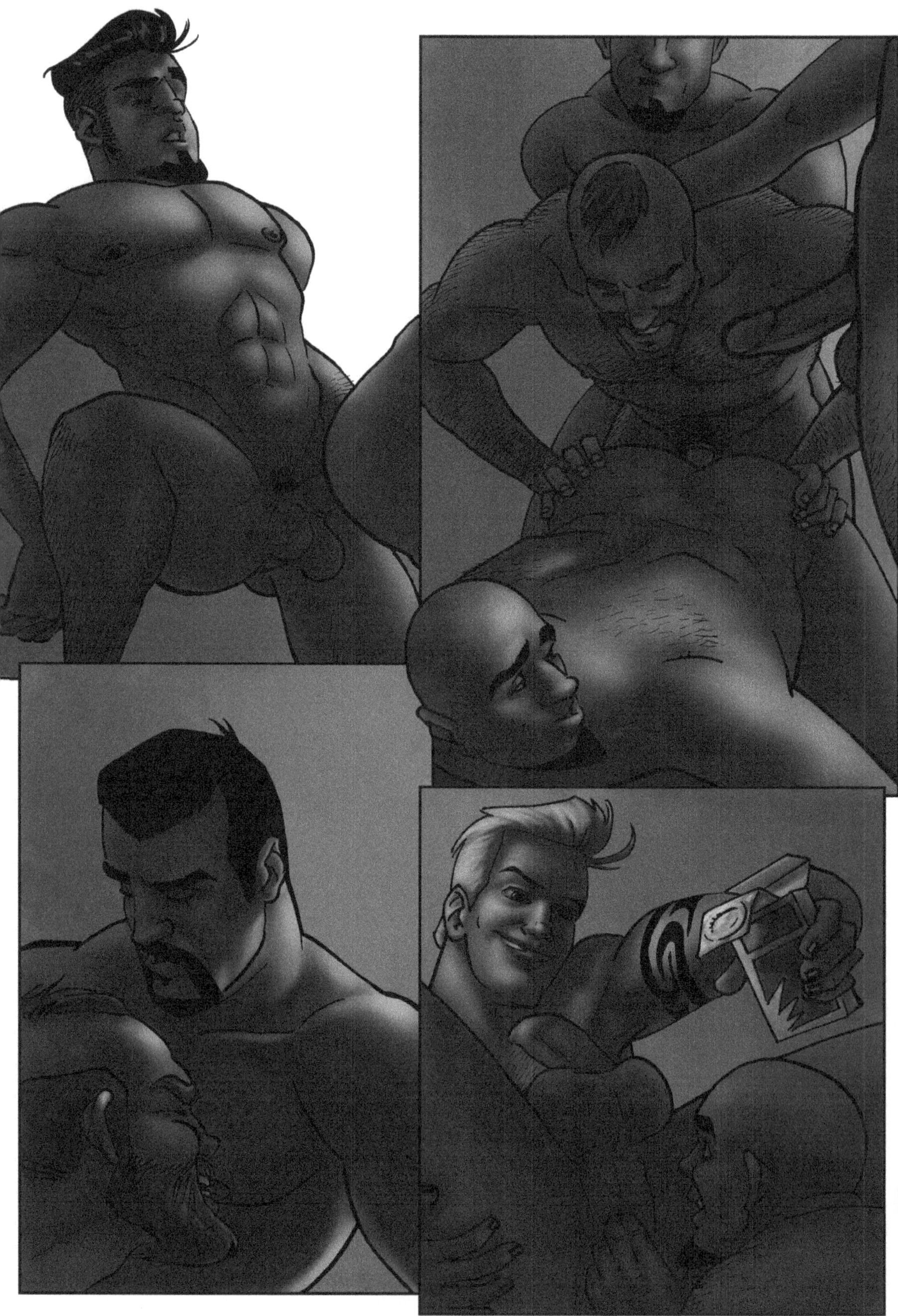

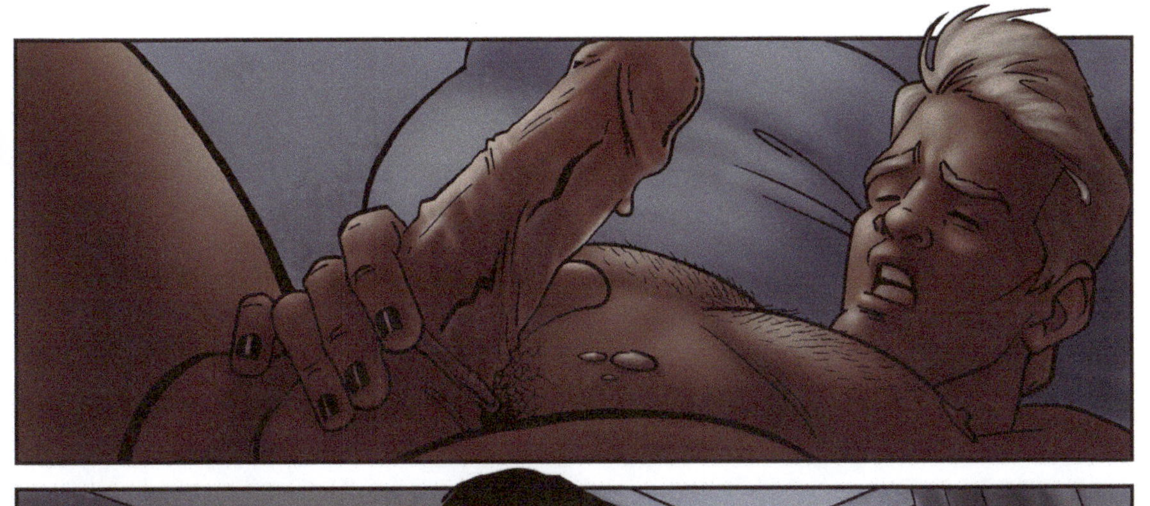

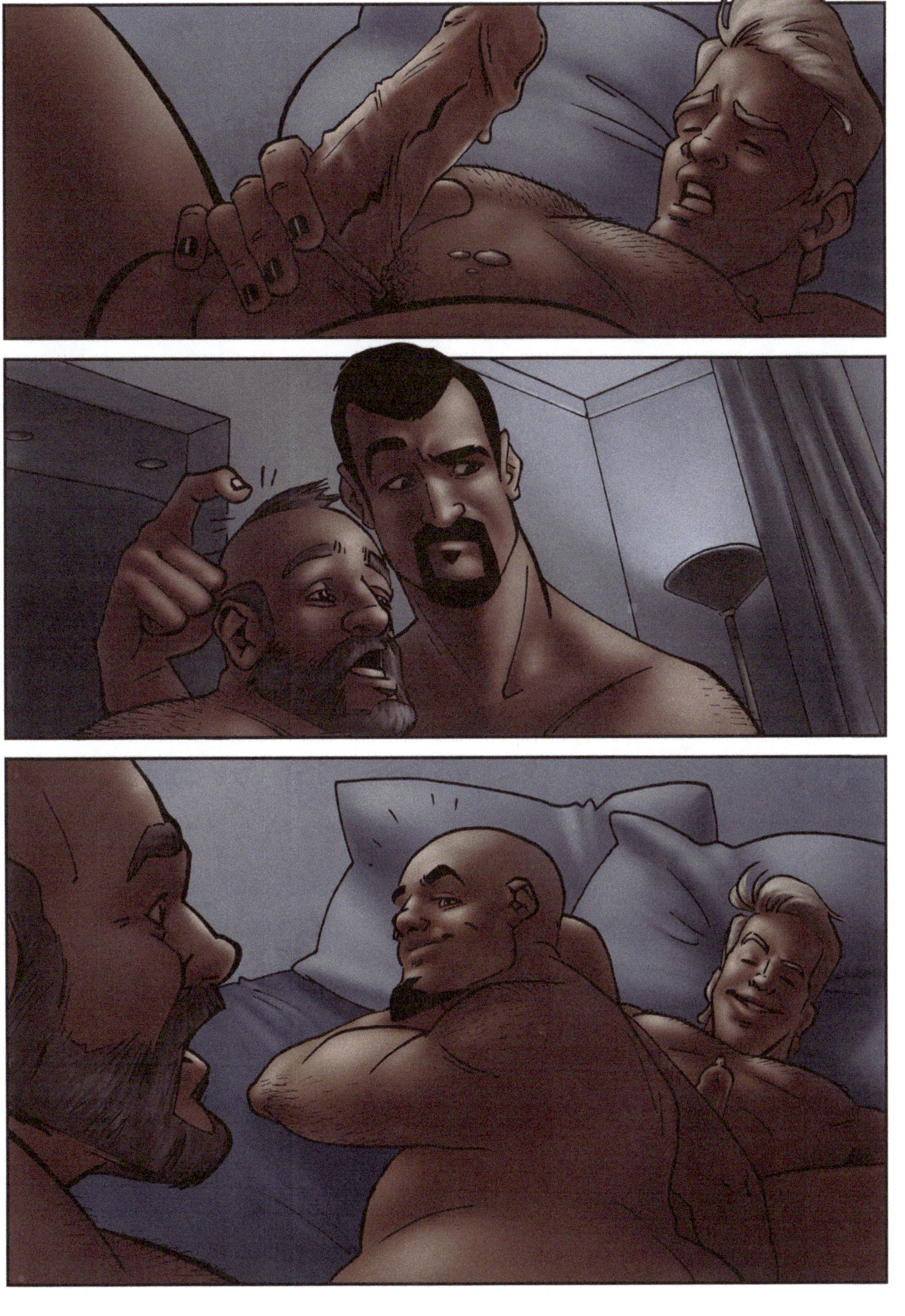

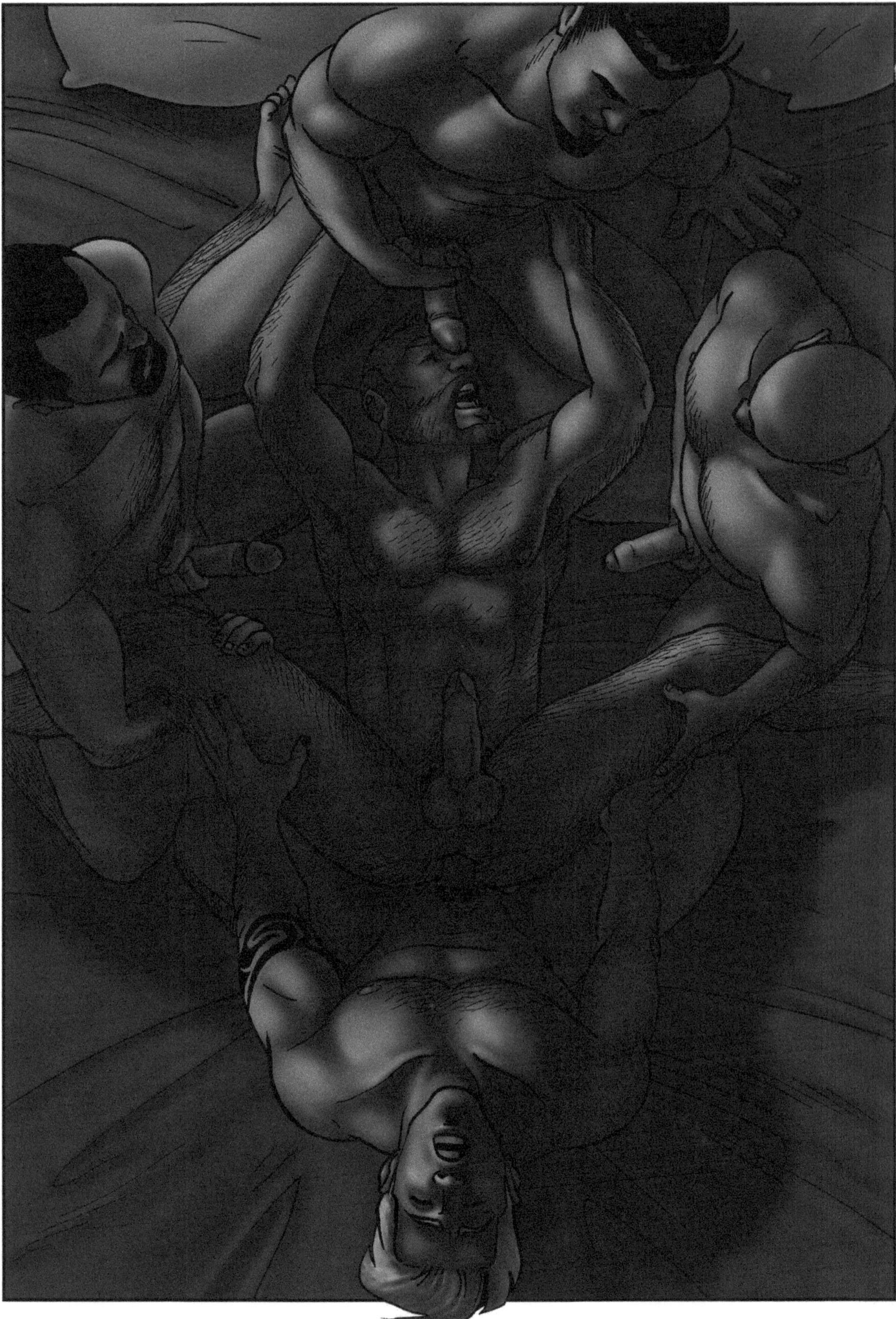

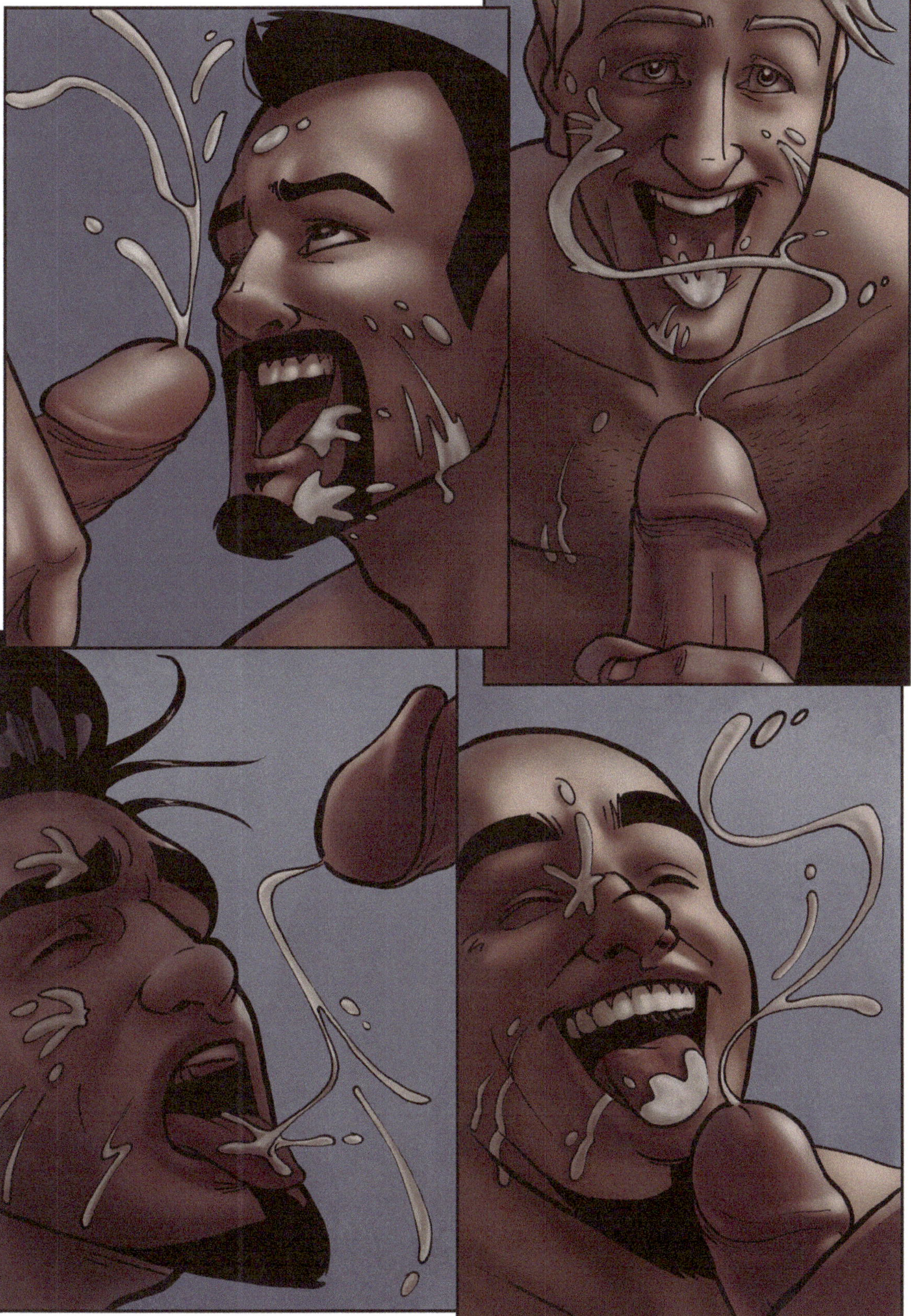

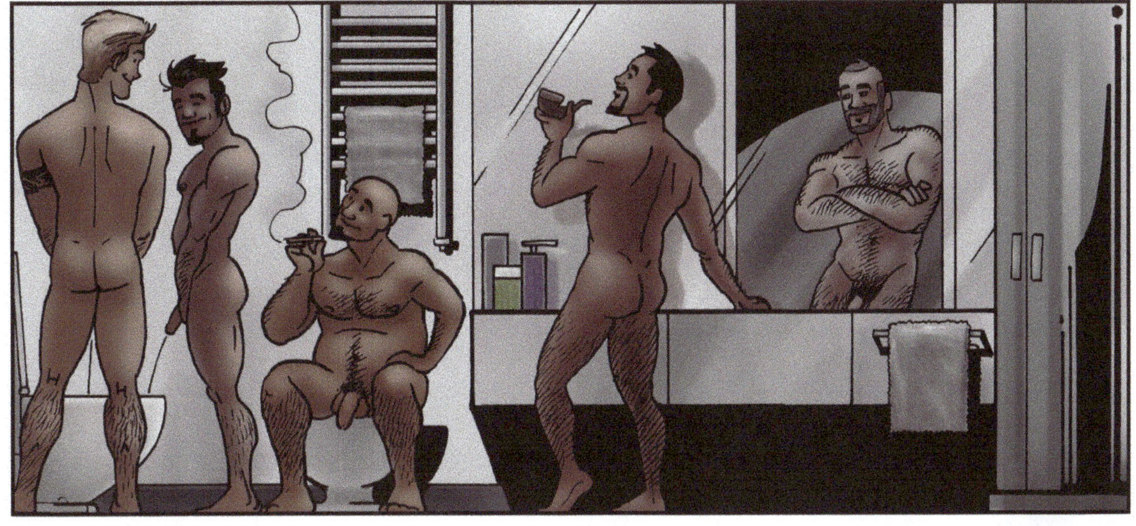

About The Authors:

<u>Dale Lazarov</u> is the writer, art director and licensor of Sticky Graphic Novels -- wordless, gay character-based, sex-positive graphic novels for an international audience that are considered "a joyous expression of male/male sexuality that, while erotic, is neither grubby nor tasteless" (*The Novel Approach*). Since 2006, he has collaborated on 12 hardcover Sticky Graphic Novels and 39 digital editions with distinctive and evocative gay comics artists from around the globe. He lives in Chicago.

<u>Mauro "Maureeno" Mariotti</u> was born in Tuscany just in time to catch the full 80's and started to draw at two years old, so an art school was the obvious path to follow. He decided to study at Scuola Internazionale di Comics in Florence, before starting a series of experiences in search of a good place to fit himself in: painting, set design for TV, decoration, illustration, comics, always driven and influenced by his passionate love for cinema, music, art and hunger for people. He is still searching.

<u>Janos Janecki</u> is an artist, graphic designer and web developer. He studied law but later decided to go on a creative track and studied advertising. Janos first started drawing digitally in 2004 and has been building a practice in graphic design and art since then. Traditional art and literature have always been his major interests and source of inspiration along with developing interests in nature, interior design, languages, culture, state-of-the-art technology and human enhancement. Visit his website at janeckistudio.com.

www.ingramcontent.com/pod-product-compliance
Lightning Source LLC
Chambersburg PA
CBHW051119300726
48981CB00002B/192